I HAVE SCHOOLWORK TO DO
JOSEPH PONDER
ILLUSTRATED BY ARNOLD SPIKES

I Have Schoolwork to Do

Joseph Ponder

Illustrated by Arnold Spikes

Acknowledgments

I would like to first thank my Lord and Savior Jesus Christ who gave me mytalent. Then I would like to thank my mom, Ruby Ponder, my African Queen, who supports me in all that I do. And, I must not forget my children, Alexandria Ponder, Lucky Cox, Sanquita Cox, Maylik Ponder, and my deceased son, Sergio Marciano Cox Ponder. This book is dedicated to Sergio who was brutally murdered 11/2016.

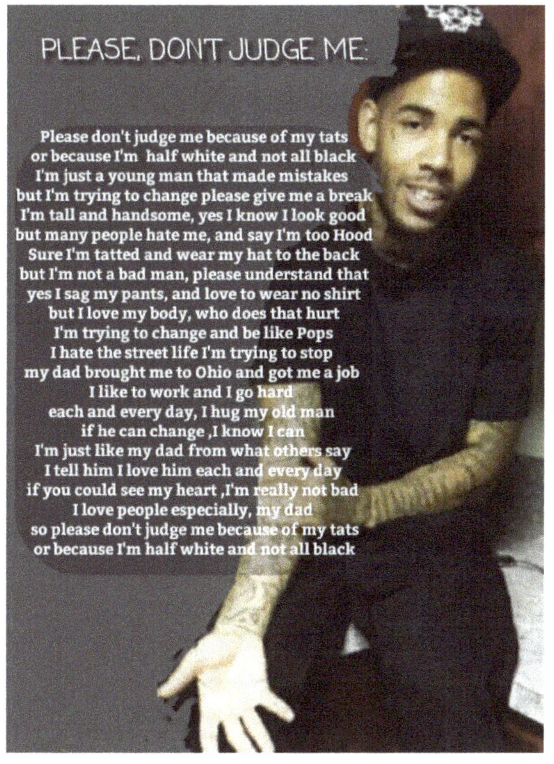

Lastly, the others that truly support me, Mr. Don Laubenthal, Mr. Eris Welch (Coach), Mrs A. Perkins, Zack, Mr. Stevens, and the entire Sports & Exercise Dept. at Columbus State Community College. Then there is Jessica M. Richardson, Faye Ray, Jacque Dixon, Charlene Anderson, Mr. Dwight Ware, John Hemming, Steve Clark, Teri Wise, Clark Kellogg, Dr. Rodney Harrelson, Marcello Myers, Kevin Spheres, First Church of God, Freedom Reign Christian Center, Trazz Sawyer, and Mr. Dan Good. If I've forgotten anyone that has supported me, please place your names here:

____

____

____

____

____

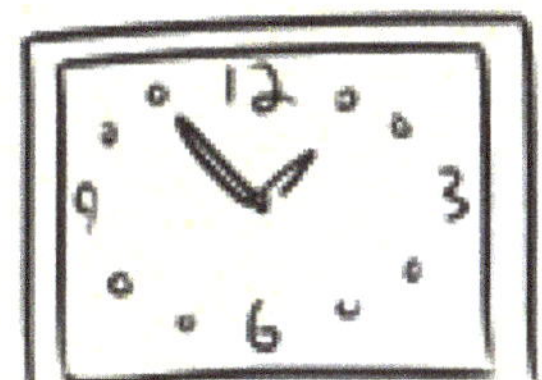

I am the young girl,
That the boys say is **fine**.

They ask for my number,
All requests I **DECLINE**

Joseph Ponder

I'm not **conceited**,
I'm no better than you.
But, I am an honor student,
And I have **schoolwork** to do.

Hey, Lil' Sue
How do you do?
Are you busy right now?
May I speak with you?

Joseph Ponder
A+
I'm sorry, Cass
But, I'm late for class.
I have a test
I have to pass.

Ok, Lil' Sue
I'm watching you.
You're always busy with
Schoolwork to do.

Lil' Sue **smiled**.
Then shook her head.
She could **care less**
To what that boy had said.

She **passed** her test.
What an easy task.

She grabbed her bookbag,
Then **departed** to class.

Hey Lil' Sue, don't you
Forget I'm watching you.
I'm Cass baby,

     And I like you too.
     I'm **tired** of hearing that
     You have **schoolwork** to do.

Sue was really **tired**
Of the kid called Cass.
She **hated** being followed
From class to class.

Please, Cass.
I **won't** date you.
I told you before,
I have **schoolwork** to do.

I'm asking you, Cass
Go **bother** another.
Don't make me call
My big **brother**

Cass didn't **care,**
He kept making passes.
He followed Lil' Sue
To all her classes.

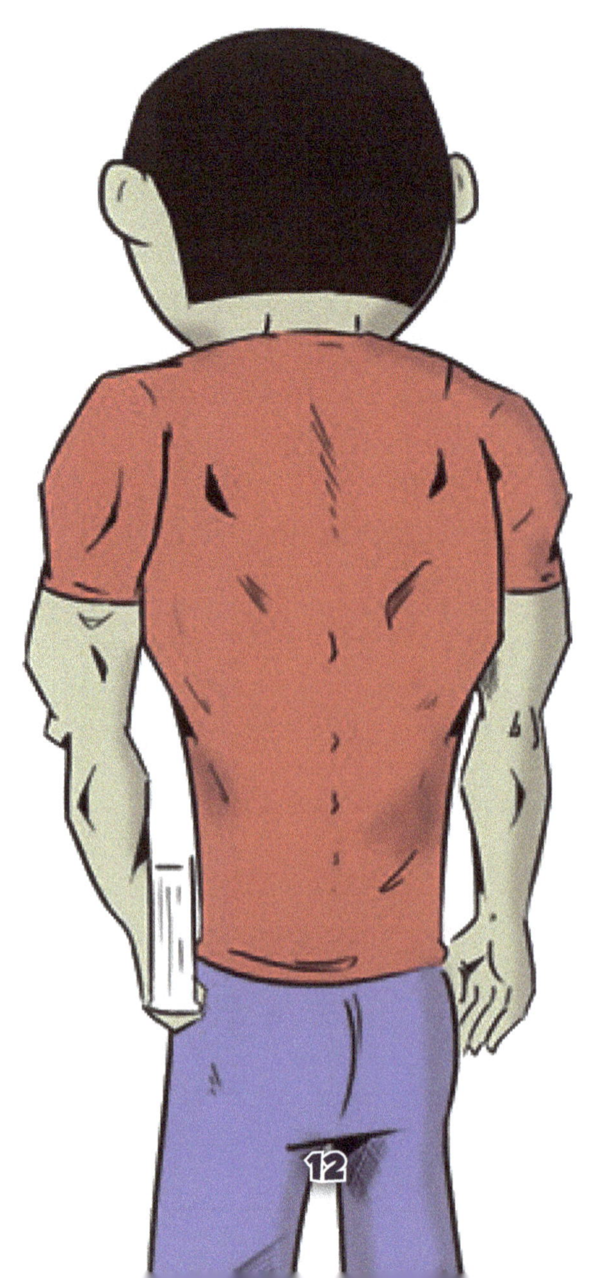

Then the day came
When Sue's brother, Joe Pool
Made his presence
Known t o Sue's school.

All the kids
Had heard of
Joe Pool.
They were all shocked
That he came to their
school.

Sue and her brother
Walked from
class to **class**.

Then, at last,
They stumbled unto
Cas

Joe Pool approached
The big, young child.

He wanted no problems,
Just to talk awhile.

Joe Pool spoke
In a very **calm** manner.

But Cass could see a
monster, Not Mr. Banner.

Joseph Ponder

Cass still liked Lil' Sue
Yet, he stayed away.
His stalking days were through

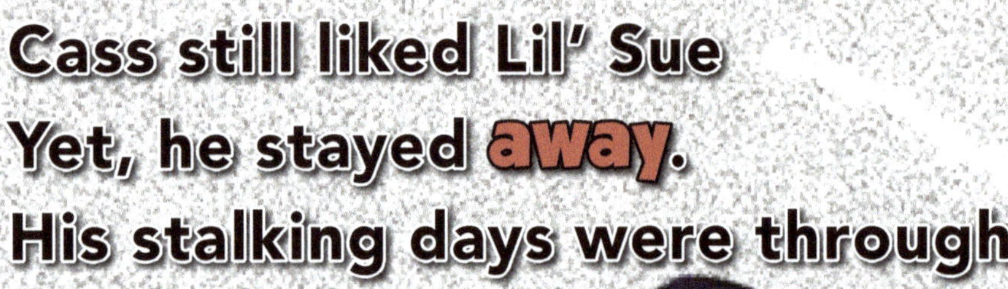

So, Lil' Sue kept
studying hard.
She only received A's
on her report card.

She's the pretty girl
That boys came to.
But, she always told them
'I have schoolwork to do.'

Joseph Ponder

Summer **passed**
The next year came
Cass was **different**
No longer the same.

Each day he saw Sue
She was **rushing** to class
The word was still out
Getting **A's** was her task

He **respected** Sue
For her attitude towards school
Even her brother
Who kept his **cool**

Each class he took
He'd **study** hard
He wanted good **grades**
On his report card.

Joseph Ponder

To his surprise
They had become pals
He had to admit
She was quite a gal.

They laughed and joked
About the issues of the past
They wanted a friendship
That they knew would last.

So, **Sue** and **Cass**
Both studied hard
They both received **A's**
On their report cards

Joseph Ponder

Cass followed Sue's **motto**
She did too
They both told friends
'We Have Schoolwork to Do!'

www.ingramcontent.com/pod-product-compliance
Lightning Source LLC
Chambersburg PA
CBHW041145300726
48978CB00016B/1388